Little Red Robin

We Are Super!

Do you have all the Little Red Robin books?

- ☐ Buster's Big Surprise
- ☐ The Purple Butterfly
- ☐ How Bobby Got His Pet
- ☐ We are Super!
- ☐ New Friends
- ☐ Robo-Robbie

Also available as ebooks

If you feel ready to read a longer book,
look out for more stories about Jonny and Tommy

Little Red
Robin

Guy Bass
Illustrated by Jamie Littler

SCHOLASTIC

For Cosimo and Felix

Scholastic Children's Books
An imprint of Scholastic Ltd
Euston House, 24 Eversholt Street
London, NW1 1DB, UK
Registered office: Westfield Road, Southam, Warwickshire, CV47 0RA
SCHOLASTIC and associated logos are trademarks and/or registered
trademarks of Scholastic Inc.

First published in 2014 by Scholastic Ltd

ISBN 978 1407 13884 8

A CIP catalogue record for this book is available from the British Library

Printed in China.

1 3 5 7 9 10 8 6 4 2

www.scholastic.co.uk/zone
www.guybass.com

Chapter One

Jonny and Tommy were twins. They looked exactly the same, except for their hair. Jonny's was blond and neat.

Tommy's was a messy black mop.

The boys lived with their dad in a big, invisible house on top of a mountain.

Their dad was away a lot, so their uncle and aunt looked after them.

Uncle Dogday
was a talking dog.

Aunt Sandwich
was a talking
hamster.

"Eat up, boys – breakfast is the most important meal of the day," said Uncle Dogday, trotting into the kitchen. "Who'd like a dog biscuit? They've got everything a growing pup needs. . ."

"The boys need people food, you dopey dog," chuckled Aunt Sandwich. She scurried up on to the table. "Do you fancy a chestnut, boys? I've been keeping them nice and warm in my cheeks. . ."

Jonny pulled a face. "I think I'll have cereal," he replied.

"Toast for me," added Tommy with a grimace.

"You boys – so similar yet so different!" giggled Aunt Sandwich, turning on the radio.

"Hey, where's Dad?" Jonny asked. "He said he was going to spend the day with us. He promised."

"Breaking news!" said a loud radio announcer.
"A giant flying robot octopus is attacking the city!
Who can stop its rampage? Who will save the day?
But wait, what's this? A lone figure, streaking
through the sky . . . why, it's Captain Atomic!"

"Dad!" cried Jonny and Tommy together.

They listened as their dad, Captain Atomic, the world's greatest superhero, did battle with the giant flying robot octopus.

"Dad isn't going to spend the day with us, is he?" sighed Jonny.

"I'm sorry, boys," replied Uncle Dogday. "I'm afraid your father had to leave early for work."

"It's always the same," grumbled Jonny. "Whenever Dad says he's going to spend time with us, he ends up having to save the day instead."

"I wish we had superpowers," moaned Tommy. "Then we could go with Dad on his adventures instead of being stuck here."

"Being a superhero is about more than just having superpowers," said Uncle Dogday. "If you ever get superpowers of your own, you'll learn that."

"Yeah, but—" began Tommy.

"No buts," replied Uncle Dogday. "Now, why don't you go and play in the garden?"

Chapter Two

Jonny and Tommy had been in the garden all
morning. It was their favourite place on the
mountain. The garden was as big as a football
pitch and had a swing and a slide. It was also full
of fun things that their dad had brought back from
his adventures. There was a broken ninja robot, a
bashed-up tank and even a crashed flying saucer.

But today, all the boys could think about was their dad.

"Dad never spends any time with us," huffed Tommy, as Jonny pushed him on the swing.

"Why can't the world save itself for once? It's not fair!" growled Jonny, pushing the swing hard.

Tommy was suddenly sent flying! He zoomed
high into the air and disappeared into the clouds.

"AAAAH!" cried Tommy as he whooshed up into the sky. After a moment he stopped screaming and looked down. He had stopped . . . in mid-air.

"Hey, I'm not falling!" he said. "Am I floating? No . . . I'm flying! Which means. . ."

Tommy flew back towards the garden. He spotted Jonny and swooped towards him.

"Look out below!" he cried.

"AAH!" screamed Jonny, as his brother whizzed past his head. "How are you doing that?"

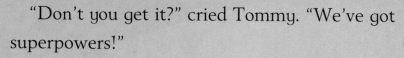

"Don't you get it?" cried Tommy. "We've got superpowers!"

"Superpowers? You mean—" began Jonny.

"I mean we're superheroes!" cried Tommy. "We can go out saving the day with Dad! We can do anything!"

Chapter Three

Suddenly, Tommy grabbed Jonny by the arm and lifted him high into the air!

"What are you doing?" cried Jonny as Tommy
spun, swooped and loop-de-looped. "Put me down!"

"You asked for it," chuckled Tommy. He dropped Jonny on top of the slide. Jonny slid down it and skidded along the ground.

Then he got to his feet, laughing.

"That ... was awesome," he chuckled. "Now it's my turn!"

Jonny picked up the slide and threw it at Tommy.

Tommy whizzed out of the way of the soaring slide.

"Missed!" he laughed.

"Dodge this," said Jonny. He flung the ninja robot but Tommy darted out of the way again.

Next, the bashed-up tank flew past Tommy's ears and smashed into the ground.

Finally, Jonny picked up the crashed flying saucer and flung it like a frisbee! Tommy squealed and flew out of the way.

The flying saucer spun through the sky . . . and
landed with a KRASSH! – on the roof of the house.

"Uh-oh – that's not good," said Tommy as he landed on the ground. A moment later, Uncle Dogday and Aunt Sandwich came racing out of the house.

"Tommy! Jonny!" yelled Uncle Dogday. "What was that noise? What on Earth is going on?"

28

Jonny was about to confess everything when Tommy interrupted.

"Aliens are attacking! They crashed their spaceship into the roof – look!" Tommy said, quickly. "It was nothing to do with us!"

"Oh me, oh my! An invasion!" cried Aunt Sandwich. "Get inside, quickly!"

"It's too late!" cried Uncle Dogday, pointing a paw into the air. "Look, up in the sky!"

Jonny and Tommy looked up. A huge metal shape was soaring through the air towards them.

"AAH! Giant flying robot octopus!" they screamed.

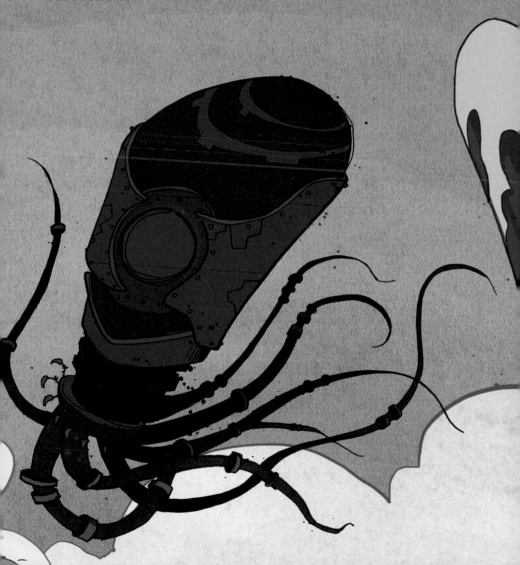

"Don't panic, everyone," said a loud, deep voice. "This thing's out of action for good."

It was Captain Atomic. He was carrying the giant flying robot octopus in one hand as he soared through the air.

"Dad!" cried the boys. Captain Atomic landed in the garden and placed the octopus on the ground in front of them.

"I thought it might make a nice present. Sorry I didn't have time to wrap it," he said.

"Oh me, oh my, there's still an alien invasion to worry about," said Aunt Sandwich. "A flying saucer just crashed on to the roof!"

"Is that so?" replied Captain Atomic. He looked at the mess in the garden. Then he stared at Jonny and Tommy. "Do you know anything about this, boys?"

"Well, um, we—" began Jonny, shuffling his feet.

"It was nothing to do with us!" interrupted Tommy. "There's no way we could have done all this, not unless we had superpowers . . . which we don't. . ."

"Really?" said Captain Atomic. "Then would you care to explain why you're floating above the ground?"

Tommy looked down. He was hovering in the air but he hadn't even noticed.

Chapter Four

As it happened, everyone was so delighted that the boys had their own superpowers that they didn't really mind about all the damage.

Captain Atomic gave his boys a hug and said, "I'm sorry I had to dash off this morning. And I'm sure you'll make great superheroes one day."

Then they settled down with a bowl of double-nut ice cream (Aunt Sandwich's favourite) and watched the Funny Bunny Cartoon Comedy Hour on TV.

"We interrupt Funny Bunny Cartoon Comedy Hour to bring you a news flash!" said the loud newsreader.

"Now what?" grumbled Tommy.

40

"A fire-breathing ghost dinosaur is attacking the city!" continued the newsreader. "Who will save the city? Who will save the day?"

"This sounds like a job for Captain Atomic," said the boys' dad as he got to his feet. "Save me some ice cream, will you?"

LAUNCH PAD

"We'll come with you!" cried Tommy.

"Yeah, we're superheroes too now!" added Jonny.

"Sorry, boys – there's a lot more to being a superhero than just having superpowers," replied Captain Atomic. "Plus, you dropped a flying saucer on to the roof. You have a lot of cleaning up to do."

And with that, Captain Atomic dashed off to save the day.

"You heard your father – time to tidy up that mess you made," huffed Uncle Dogday.

Jonny and Tommy sighed. Then they looked at each other and began to smile.

"Can we use our superpowers?"